For Maureen Poland – M.W.

To Bill and Irene – J.C.

ORCHARD BOOKS
Carmelite House
50 Victoria Embankment
London EC4Y 0DZ

First published in hardback in Great Britain 2004

This edition first published in 2015

ISBN 978 1 40834 153 7

Text © Martin Waddell 2004

Illustrations © Jason Cockcroft 2004

The rights of Martin Waddell to be identified as the author and of Jason Cockcroft to be
identified as the illustrator of this work have been asserted by them in accordance with the
Copyright, Designs and Patents Act, 1988.

A CIP catalogue record for this book is available from the British Library.

2 4 6 8 10 9 7 5 3 1

Printed in China

Orchard Books
An imprint of Hachette Children's Group
Part of The Watts Publishing Group Limited
An Hachette UK Company
www.hachette.co.uk

Room *for a* Little One

Martin Waddell ✳ Jason Cockcroft

ORCHARD

It was a cold winter's night.
Kind Ox lay in his stable,
close to the side of the inn.

Old Dog came by.

He stopped, and looked into the stable.

"I need somewhere to rest," said Old Dog.

"Come inside," Kind Ox said.

"There's always room for a little one here."

Old Dog came in and lay down in the straw.

He nestled close to Kind Ox,

sharing the warmth of his stable.

Stray Cat peered in.

She saw Old Dog and she stopped.

Stray Cat arched her back and her fur bristled.

"I'll not chase you," said Old Dog.

"Come inside," Kind Ox said.

"There's always room for a little one here."

Stray Cat came into the stable.

She curled up in the straw,

close to the friends she had found,

purring and twitching her tail.

Small Mouse stopped at the door of the stable.

She saw Stray Cat and she quivered with fear.

"You're safe here, I won't harm you," said Stray Cat.

"Come inside," Kind Ox said.

"There's always room for a little one here."

Small Mouse scurried in.

She nestled down warm in the straw,

in the peace of the stable.

Then Tired Donkey came.

Joseph led him along.

Mary rode on Tired Donkey's back.

Joseph was cold and Mary was weary,

but there was no room at the inn.

"Where will my baby be born?" Mary asked.

"Come inside," Kind Ox called to Tired Donkey.

"There's always room for a little one here."

Tired Donkey brought Mary into the stable.

Joseph made her a warm bed in the straw,

to save her from the cold of the night.

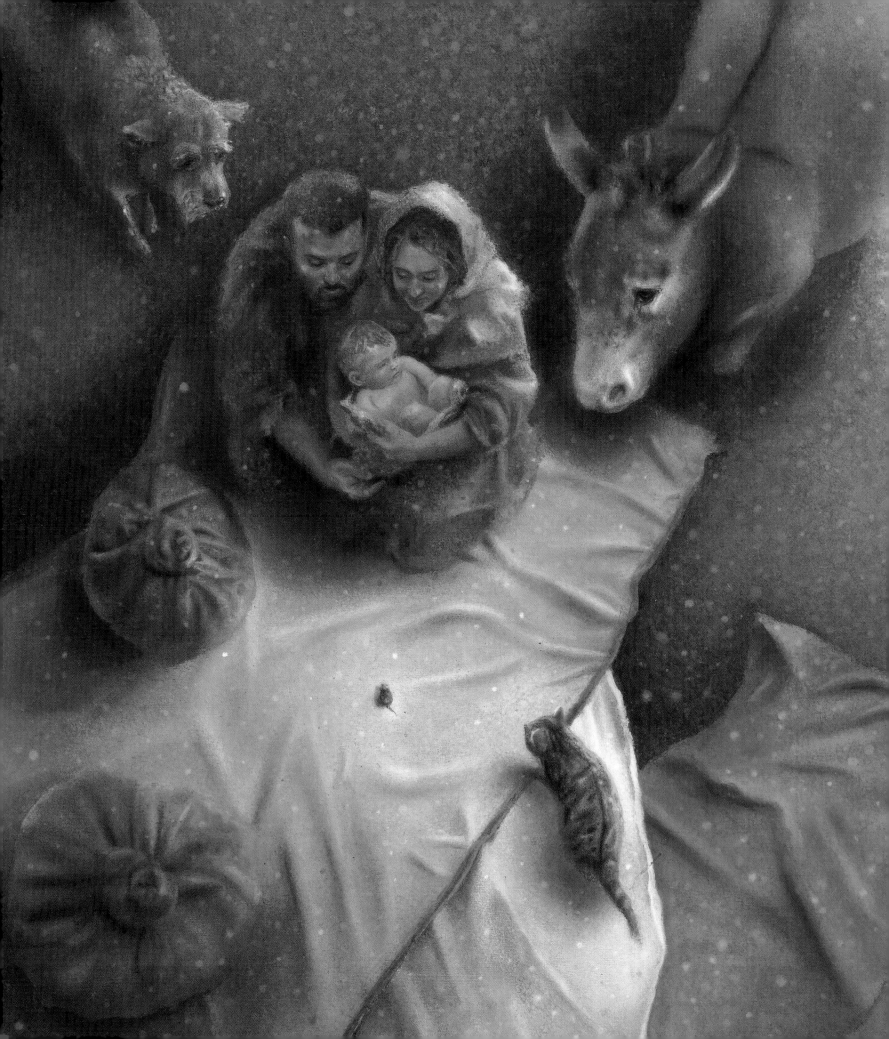

And so Jesus was born with the animals around Him;
Kind Ox, Old Dog, Stray Cat, Small Mouse, and
Tired Donkey all welcomed Him to the
warmth of their stable.

That cold winter's night,
beneath the star's light ...

...a Little One came for the world.